Orca currents

Eric Walters

ORCA BOOK PUBLISHERS

Library and Archives Canada Cataloguing in Publication

Walters, Eric, 1957-

Laggan Lard Butts / Eric Walters.

(Orca currents)

ISBN 1-55143-531-4 (bound) ISBN 1-55143-518-7 (pbk.)

I. Title. II. Series.

PS8595.A598L33 2006   jC813'.54   C2006-900468-4

Summary: Sometimes a joke can go too far.

First published in the United States, 2006
Library of Congress Control Number: 2006921145

Orca Book Publishers gratefully acknowledges the support for its publishing
programs provided by the following agencies: the Government of Canada
through the Book Publishing Industry Development Program (BPIDP), the
Canada Council for the Arts, and the British Columbia Arts Council.

Cover design: Lynn O'Rourke
Cover photography: Dayle Sutherland

Orca Book Publishers
PO Box 5626, Stn. B
Victoria, BC Canada
V8R 6S4

Orca Book Publishers
PO Box 468
Custer, WA USA
98240-0468

www.orcabook.com
Printed and bound in Canada
Printed on 50% post-consumer recycled paper,
processed chlorine free using vegetable, low VOC inks.

09 08 07 06 • 5 4 3 2 1

To all the Lard Butts in the world!

Author Note

I had just finished a presentation at Laggan public school and was fielding questions from the students. One of them asked me, "What would you write about if you were a teacher here?" I looked over at the mural on the wall of the gym—it said, *The Laggan Lairds.* Right there, in front of an audience of one hundred kids, I outlined the plot that became this novel. Go, Lard Butts!

Other titles by Eric Walters

chapter one

"Backdoor! Backdoor!" I screamed as I saw the play develop.

My teammate, Cody, turned and stared at me with an openmouthed look of confusion on his face as his man went backdoor and scored an easy lay-up.

I opened my mouth to say something, but I stopped myself. Coach had been pretty clear what he'd do if I said anything rude to anybody during the game. I bit my tongue and went to take the inbound pass while everybody else ran to the other end of the court.

Taylor—or was it Tanner?—was ready to toss it in to me. No it *was* Taylor. I'd known the twins for nine years—we'd met the first day of kindergarten—but I still had trouble telling them apart at a glance.

"That was pretty impressive, Sam," Taylor said as he tossed the ball in.

"You thought that play was impressive?" I asked in shock.

"Not the play. You keeping your mouth shut *about* Cody's play. Don't waste your time with Cody," he said under his breath as we started up the court. "The only back door Cody knows is the one that leads to his kitchen."

I fought back a laugh. Cody was a little weight challenged, but then again, the whole team, except for me and the twins, was challenged in more ways than one.

I dribbled across center. The other team had pressed all through the first half and then stopped. That was only good sportsmanship. They were up by so many points that it would have been rubbing it in to continue to press.

They knew they couldn't lose. We all knew that. I'd long ago given up any thoughts of actually winning. Come to think about it I don't think I had those thoughts even before the game had started. All I wanted was not to lose too badly.

"Three!" I yelled out.

Taylor and Tanner reacted instantly, while Cody and Travis bumped into each other trying to get to the same place. I felt like screaming directions at them—or yelling something else—but what was the point? Neither of them was very good, but they were actually the fourth-and fifth-best players on the team. We didn't have a bench. No we *did* have a bench, but the people sitting *on* the bench couldn't play basketball to save their lives.

Tanner cut around the screen. I knew it was Tanner because I saw the number on the back of his jersey. I sent the ball in, and he stopped and popped a shot. It dropped for a basket!

The crowd gave a big cheer. I turned and scowled at them. It wasn't our home game. We were so pathetic that the other team's fans were cheering for us. Pity applause. I wanted to say something to them as well. I looked down and saw our coach and my homeroom teacher, Mr. Davidson, and I shut up—again. I put my head down and ran back to our end.

"Zone two!" I called out, setting our defense.

There was no point in chasing them for the last two minutes of the game. Victory was way out of reach. If we didn't pressure them maybe they wouldn't try to score. We could at least make it harder for them to backdoor Cody again.

Their point guard stayed up high, away from the paint, eating up time. They didn't need to score, and, to be honest, I was happy if nobody scored. I just wanted the game to end so the score wouldn't get any more lopsided.

"Campbell!" Coach Davidson called out. He always called us by our last names during the games. "Pressure the ball!"

Obviously he thought we weren't losing badly enough, because he couldn't possibly think we could win. Nobody could be that stupid.

I moved out toward the ball carrier. He turned his back and used his body to shield the ball. He kept on dribbling. I wasn't getting any closer. Let him dribble out the clock.

He looked over his shoulder at me. "What's a laird?"

His question, in the middle of the game, caught me by surprise. "Um...it's the name of our school team."

"I know that, it's on the uniforms. I just wanted to know what a laird was. What does it mean?"

"It's Scottish. It's some sort of weapon, I think, something they used when there were knights and armor."

He passed the ball off. "Lairds," he chuckled. "Your team should be the *Laggan lard butts*."

He suddenly broke for the net, cutting by me before I could react. He got the ball back and drove for the open net and an easy bucket. I pushed him from behind with both hands, sending him sailing through the air. He landed face-first on the ground and—

The ref blew his whistle to signal the foul. At the same time Coach Davidson yelled for a time-out.

I walked over to the bench. I knew what was going to happen.

"Campbell, you're—"

"I know, I know, I'm on the bench."

That was the end of the game for me, but it really didn't matter. With or without me we'd already lost. Probably better this way, I thought. Now all I had to do was keep my mouth shut for the next two minutes. Say nothing to my coach, or my teammates, the other team, the ref or the fans. Just shut up and be a good loser. Since practice makes perfect you'd think that I'd know how to be a good loser by now. I should be a *perfect* loser by now.

Our school teams always lost. It didn't matter what sport—basketball, soccer, baseball, volleyball or hockey—we sucked at them all. I'd been on all our school teams every year since grade six, and we'd never had a winning team. Forget winning team, we'd hardly ever had a win.

One of our rare wins had been the first basketball game of the season. We'd won by ten points. We'd played well. We were good. At least that's what I had thought. What I didn't know then was that the first team we'd played was just more terrible than we were. They lost every game all season, including the two against us. Those were our only wins.

Winning that first game made the season even worse. It had given me hope. It wasn't good to have hope when your team played hopelessly.

The buzzer sounded, mercifully ending the game. I stood up but didn't look at the score clock. I joined my team and shuffled toward center court to congratulate the winners.

"Not bad," Tanner said as he came up beside me.

"We were terrible."

"Not the game. You. You almost made it through an entire game without losing it."

"My proudest moment."

"Just be polite in the line," Taylor said as he joined us. "Don't let them get you going."

"I'll be polite."

"Good, 'cause we need you to play the last game of the year."

Earlier in the year, during the lineup at the end of a game, I'd been in an argument that almost led to a fight with a player from the other team. I was told that if that happened again I'd be suspended from the team for the rest of the year.

I walked through the line, slapping hands and mumbling "good game" as the other team did the same. I kept my head down. I didn't want to look at anybody. I knew everybody on that team—most by name. You play against people for three years and you get to know them. Three years of playing. Three years of losing.

We walked back toward the bench.

"What did that guy say to you?" Tanner asked.

"Somebody said something to me?" I

asked as I skidded to a stop. "Somebody in line said something to me?"

"Not in line, during the game...at the end."

"Oh, him. He said that our team should be called the Lard Butts."

Tanner started laughing.

"You think that's funny?" I demanded.

"Of course I do. Think about how we play. Maybe we should be the Lard Butts. Forget it, let's get changed and get out of this place."

There was no argument from me. I wanted out as soon as possible. Maybe I wasn't a good loser, but I wanted to be a loser who didn't hang around.

chapter two

We piled into Mr. Davidson's van. Probably the best thing about having him as coach was that he was the only teacher with a van big enough to carry a whole basketball team. It was a fifteen-seater. He used it to drive people to and from church on Sundays. He was a big-time church-going sort of guy—not that there was anything wrong with that.

He was also a pretty good teacher and a nice guy, but he knew next to nothing about basketball. That was okay, though, because he knew he didn't know much and he didn't try to tell us what to do. He just let us call our own plays and play the game.

"Everybody buckle up!" he sang out.

Seatbelts clicked through the vehicle.

"Now that we're all safe we can go."

He put the van into gear and we started away. I looked back at the school. This was the last time I would ever have to come here to lose, I thought. The last time I'd ever have to drag myself out of Maple Ridge school after losing another game to the Maple Ridge Mustangs. I *hated* that school.

They were everything we weren't. We were little and they were big. They were city and we were country. They were winners and we were...well, we all knew what the score was.

At least this year those stupid Mustangs weren't going to win it all. It looked like they were going to finish second. They had lost both of their games with the other big city school. Not that I necessarily liked that team any better.

"I'm really proud of you boys!" Mr. Davidson called out over the sound of the engine.

I had to hand it to him. He never got down. He always seemed to be able to find the silver lining in any cloud—even a storm cloud.

"Can you imagine how much prouder you'd be if we'd won the game?" Tanner asked.

"Wouldn't make any difference. First place or eighth, I'm just as proud. It isn't whether you win or lose—"

"It's how you play the game!" we yelled back, cutting him off.

I don't know how many times we'd heard him say that. Certainly a lot more times than the number of wins we'd had.

"And, who knows, we might still win it all," he said.

"How do you figure that?" Taylor asked.

"We are solidly in seventh place."

Great, seventh place in an eight-team league. Made me feel proud.

"And our last game is against the team

that is just ahead of us in the standings. Martintown," Mr. Davidson said. We'd lost to Martintown by only two points in our first meeting. That game had been a heart-breaker. It was better to lose by a lot than by a little. "If we beat them we'll finish in sixth place."

"Sixth place, my dream," I said sarcastically.

"We're number six! We're number six!" Tanner started chanting and the whole van—except me—joined in.

"And!" Mr. Davidson said, silencing the cheer, "if we finish sixth that means we make the play-offs."

"That would be great!" somebody said.

Yeah, right, great.

"Who would we play in the first round?" I asked.

"I think sixth place plays the team in first place."

There was sudden silence from everybody. We all knew what that meant. If we did make the play-offs our last game was going to be a blowout of epic size. Go, Lairds, go.

"I think we do really well," Mr. Davidson said, "relative to the size of our school. We're so much smaller than every other school in the league."

He did have a point. Martintown had over eight hundred kids. We had one hundred and fifty kids between kindergarten and grade eight. We had ten grades with an average of fifteen kids per grade. I didn't even know what it was like to not be in a split class. Martintown had more grade seven and eight kids than we had in our entire school. More kids tried out for the teams and that usually meant there were more kids who could play well.

I looked around the bus. We had ten kids on the team. Three of us could play basketball. Everybody else had a vague idea at best. It wasn't really their fault. Cody couldn't play basketball to save his life, but he was a great hockey player—a goalie. He was a lot better at hockey than I was, a lot better than any of us. Kevin was a great skateboarder and Kyle was a swimmer. We had lots of people who were good at something. We just didn't have enough kids who were all good at the same thing to make up a team that could win.

It also didn't help that most of us lived on farms. It wasn't as if we could get together on the street outside our houses and play pickup games. We lived miles and miles apart. There wasn't even a street where we could play. We had dirt roads. No park, no hoops, no ice. Just lots of fields.

Laggan public school sat in the middle of nowhere, surrounded on all sides by farms. I could always tell which direction the wind was blowing by the odor in the air.

If it smelled bad the wind was coming from the west, the direction of a big pig farm. I read that pigs were clean. Maybe one or two were but a few hundred certainly didn't smell clean.

If the wind blew from the east it passed the sunflower fields and was sort of sweet. When they were in bloom the smell was almost overwhelming.

From the north I could smell the city— actually I could smell the KFC at the edge of town. It was amazing how far that smell could travel, especially around lunchtime.

Wind from the south meant no smell at all.

"Mr. Davidson, I have a question," Taylor asked.

"Go ahead, shoot."

"I was wondering...and I really should know this, so it's pretty stupid."

"There are no stupid questions," Mr. Davidson said.

Only stupid people asking them, I thought, but didn't say.

"Can you tell me what a laird is?"

"Laird. It is a Scottish word."

"I knew that," I chipped in from the back.

"The whole history of our community is Scottish. That's why we have so many Campbells, and Turners, McDonalds and, of course, Davidsons."

"So what does it mean?" I asked.

"It is Scottish for lord."

"Lord, like God?" somebody asked.

"More like lord of the manor, the owner of an estate," Mr. Davidson said.

"I guess that isn't so bad."

"And most people, most of our students and teachers, say it wrong. It should be pronounced as if it were spelled l - a - r - d. We are the Laggan *Lards*."

"Lard? You mean like fat?" Tanner asked *and* gave me a funny look.

"You would say it that way, yes."

Tanner leaned close to me. "Maybe Lard Butts wasn't so far off," he said, his voice just above a whisper.

"Great, just great," I muttered. "Isn't it bad enough that we're a joke without having a stupid name?" I demanded.

"It's a name with tradition," Mr. Davidson said.

"Just like our tradition of losing," I said.

"I'm not sure that's a tradition as much as an unfortunate situation," Mr. Davidson said. "If we look at winning and losing according to the size of the school we'd definitely be winners."

"I'll keep that in mind if they ever start keeping score that way," I said.

"And do you think the name would make a difference?" Mr. Davidson asked.

"I don't know if it would make any difference, but at least the other team could only make fun of how we play and not what we're called."

"Interesting. Perhaps there is something we can do about it," Mr. Davidson said.

"You have an idea?" Taylor asked.

"Perhaps. First let me think things through. We'll talk more tomorrow in class."

chapter three

"Everybody please sit down," Mr. Davidson said.

We all stopped talking and settled into our seats.

"Before we start on our new project I want to review what we've learned so far. Let's talk about democracy. Can somebody give me a definition?"

Hands shot up around the room.

"Sarah."

"Democracy is a Greek word which means rule of the people."

"Very good."

Sarah gave her smug little smile. She thought she was never wrong about anything. The part that annoyed me the most was that she *was* almost always right. We'd been in the same class—all of us had been in the same class—since kindergarten. I'd met her on the second day of class, the day after I met the twins. With the twins it had been buddies at first sight. With Sarah it was an emotion somewhere between aggravated and annoyed. She could drive me crazy.

Sarah was a triple threat. She had been chosen to give the graduation speech, she was the student president and she was, without a doubt, the number one teacher suck-up of all time.

I was looking forward to next year. I was tired of having the same kids in my class, year after year, after year, after year. We'd all be going to the same high school, the *big* high school, but we wouldn't be alone. We would be with kids from every school around here.

There would be hundreds of kids in grade nine. Hundreds and hundreds. With my luck Sarah would be in my class and Tanner and Taylor would be in another.

"Now democracy is a Greek word... because...?" Mr. Davidson asked.

Sarah's hand shot into the air, as did a whole lot of other hands.

"Tanner?"

"Because democracy began in ancient Greece in city states."

"Like Athens," Taylor said.

They had a "twin thing" and often completed each other's sentences and thoughts. They also completed each other's plans and plots—plots that often got the three of us in trouble. We'd all spent a fair amount of time in the office this year, although I had the lead in that race.

"Yeah, it was in Athens," Tanner said. "That's where they started giving every person the right to vote."

"Not every person," Sarah said. "Every *man*."

She said "man" like it was a bad word.

She had this anti-male thing. At least she'd had that attitude since I had broken up with her two weeks earlier. She probably believed she was the one that broke up with me, but we both knew that was a pile of...

I couldn't believe I'd ever, ever gone out with her. What an idiot I'd been. Why would I date somebody who drives me crazy?

"Actually," I said as I stuck up my hand, "it wasn't any man. It was any rich man."

"Correct, Sam. Only males who owned property were allowed to vote."

"That's so unfair," Sarah said.

About as unfair was having her around all the time.

"I guess they figured that women weren't ready for the responsibility of voting," I said. "Maybe the men thought women were too busy cooking and shopping."

An "ooohhh" went up from the class. Tanner and Taylor started to applaud.

"Come on, Sam, you don't actually believe that, do you?" our teacher asked.

I had the urge to say yes, but I didn't really believe it. I shook my head.

"When *did* women finally get the right to vote?" Mr. Davidson asked.

The only hand that went up was Sarah's. He motioned to her.

"The very first place was Wyoming in 1869. That was only two thousand years after men first got the vote."

"I'm surprised it didn't take longer," Tanner said.

"And what country first gave women the vote?" Mr. Davidson asked.

Again, only Sarah's hand rose. She hadn't just done all the reading: she'd memorized all of it.

"New Zealand, 1893."

"Yes. A little country on the far side of the world was the first. We have talked about *men* and *women* getting the vote. At what age are people able to vote?"

Lots of hands went up, and Mr. Davidson motioned to Cody.

"Some places it's eighteen and in other countries nineteen, twenty, even twenty-one."

"Different ages. Is there any country that allows sixteen-year-olds to vote?"

Nobody offered an answer.

"What about thirteen-year-olds?" he asked.

I knew the answer to that. "None," I said. "Nobody would let a bunch of kids our age vote."

"That, my friend, is where you are wrong," Mr. Davidson said. "Right here, right now, you are being given the right to vote."

"We are?" Tanner asked.

"Yes. I think the best way to learn about democracy is to take part in a democratic process."

"Like when I was elected student president?" Sarah asked with that little smug smile on her face.

"I don't think that qualifies, since you were the only one who ran for the job," I pointed out.

Tanner and Taylor chuckled.

"He certainly is correct," Mr. Davidson said. "And since there was no election for a student president there was no exercise in democracy."

"So what exactly are we going to vote for in this election?" Taylor asked.

"Something we talked about yesterday."

We had talked about lots of things, but I really wasn't paying that much attention to any of it.

"On the drive back to school after the game yesterday," Mr. Davidson added.

"You mean the name of the school teams?" I asked.

He nodded his head. "Would you like to explain our conversation to those who weren't in the van?"

"I guess I could." I took a deep breath. "We were talking about how we don't like the name of our school teams."

"You don't like the Lairds?" Sarah gasped.

"No? Do you?"

"It's the name we've always used, and I'm an *athletic supporter*."

Everybody started giggling and laughing.

"I mean I support our teams."

"I figured you didn't mean you were a jock strap," I said. "But why do we have to

25

have such a stupid name? Do you even know what a Laird is?"

"Well...well it's...it's Scottish."

"So are haggis and kilts and bagpipes, but we don't have to be the Laggan Bagpipes, do we?"

"I kinda like the sound of that," Tanner joked. "The Laggan Bagpipes blow another game. That works."

"I think a different name might be better. I'm suggesting that we pick some names, discuss the pros and cons of each pick and then we hold an election for the new name."

"And whatever name we choose will actually replace the Lairds?" I asked.

"Well, we really don't have the authority to do that... This will be more like a mock election."

"Mock?" Justin asked.

"That's another word for fake," I explained. Sarah wasn't the only smart one in the room.

"I don't get it, Mr. Davidson. If you want us to experience democracy shouldn't it be real?" Tanner asked. "Shouldn't we vote for something that really matters?"

"Ideally," he agreed. "But, as I said, I can't make that decision."

"Who can?" I asked.

"Probably our principal, Mr. McGregor."

"Then maybe we should talk to him," Taylor said. The rest of the class agreed.

Mr. Davidson didn't answer right away. He was thinking. Finally he nodded his head in agreement. "Let's see what he has to say."

chapter four

"I don't know about this," I said as we walked down the hall.

"I don't know why you had to come along," Sarah said.

"Me?"

"Yes. I don't know why Mr. Davidson wanted you to be part of this delegation to the principal."

"Two people are hardly a *delegation*." It was just like Sarah to use a big word when it wasn't needed.

"I don't care if it's two people or twenty-two, I still don't understand why you had to be part of it."

"It was my idea," I said.

"Your idea? Mr. Davidson came up with it."

"But he wouldn't have thought about it if I hadn't brought up the whole name thing to begin with. I should be here."

"At least, nobody in the school has been to the office more than you, so you should know the way."

I didn't answer. I didn't react. I didn't want to give her the satisfaction.

"And you've spent so much time with the principal—I wonder, do you still call him Mr. McGregor or do you call him by his first name?"

"I don't call him by his first name, but he does like me," I said. "He likes people with backbone. Nobody likes suck-ups."

She grabbed me by the arm and spun me around. It was amazing how strong somebody that small could be.

"Are you calling me a suck-up?"

"I didn't mention any names, but you must think it applies, and if the shoe fits then—"

"Do you want me to tell you where my shoe *could* fit?" she demanded.

"Oooohhh...I'm ascared."

"Ascared isn't a word. The word is either scared or afraid, you can't put them together."

"I guess I'm just so scared and afraid that I can't talk right. I'm just so *ascared* of you that I'm making up words."

She made a strange little sound, sort of a huff, like steam escaping from a kettle. She was frustrated. I knew it would be easy to make her even more frustrated.

"The big question isn't why I'm here, but why you're part of the *delegation*. You didn't even play on any of the teams this year."

"I'm here because I'm the student president!"

"Only because nobody else wanted the job."

I could see her spine stiffen and her chest deflate all at the same time. I could always get to her, although I often felt bad after I did—like I felt now.

"Okay, how about if we stop fighting for a few minutes and get this meeting over with," I suggested.

"Let me do all the talking," Sarah said.

"Like I could stop you if I wanted. But maybe I should talk. Remember that the principal and I are tight. He was over at my house the other day watching videos and—"

"Mr. McGregor was over at your house?" she gasped.

"Sarah, I'm kidding. You do most of the talking." Since I didn't have a gag, that was a given.

We stopped at the counter in the office, and the secretary—who I thought actually ran the school—looked up at us. She gave me a scowl and Sarah a smile.

"We're here to see Mr. McGregor," Sarah said. "We have an appointment."

Appointment? Typical. Why didn't she say that her *delegation* had an appointment?

"He's expecting you," she said and motioned for us to go inside his office.

Sarah led. I followed. The door was open, but she tapped on it anyway. Mr. McGregor was sitting at his desk. He looked up from his work.

"Come in, please."

We walked in and took the two seats across from his desk. I took the seat on the left, the one closest to the door. I always took the seat closest to the door because it was two steps closer to leaving.

Instinctively I felt the palms of my hands start to sweat. I had to remind myself that I wasn't in trouble. I hadn't done anything wrong in weeks, in fact.

"Your teacher has informed me that your class has an interesting idea, a way to put your study of democracy into action."

"Yeah," I said.

"Yes, sir," Sarah replied.

What a suck-up, I thought, but I kept my mouth shut. I had the strangest thought that I should call him by his first name now, but even I wasn't *that* stupid...or brave.

"You see, sir, some of the students—not me but some of the students—don't really like the name of our school teams," Sarah continued.

"Some of us think it's stupid," I said.

Both of them shot me a dirty look.

"Well it is," I said. "Nobody knows what a laird is."

"I know what it is," Sarah said proudly.

"You know now, but you didn't this morning," I said, cutting her off right at the knees.

"Laird is certainly not a word that is used everyday," Mr. McGregor said. "But it has been the team name since the time the school was built. That is almost one hundred years of tradition."

"Tradition? Isn't that just another way of looking at the past instead of thinking about the future?" I asked.

Now they both looked shocked. I was actually a little surprised by what I'd said.

"Tradition is far more than that," said Mr. McGregor. "It is using the foundation of the past to build a future."

"Sometimes it's just saying we won't change because that's the way we have always done things. Isn't that the same argument they tried to use to exclude women from the democratic process?" I asked.

Mr. McGregor now looked shocked, and Sarah looked pleased.

"Voting has to do with it," Sarah said. "We want, as a class project, to hold an election to choose a new name for the school teams."

"Interesting idea," he said.

"So you're not against it?" I asked.

"I need to hear more before I can decide if I'm for or against this idea. Go on."

"We were thinking we could suggest possible names and then we'd vote. The name with the most votes wins," Sarah explained.

"I understand the democratic process," Mr. McGregor said with a smirk. "But are you talking about your class or the whole school?"

"Our class, I guess," Sarah said.

"And does that sound fair?" he asked.

"What do you mean?" I asked.

"Well, for one thing, half of your class, all the grade eight students, will be leaving the school in a few weeks. And second, if we just let the older students vote, aren't we doing the same thing as those who wouldn't let women have the vote?"

"Um...I guess...but even the kindergarten kids?" I asked.

"Aren't they going to spend the next nine years in this school and on those teams?" he asked.

"Yeah, I guess. So you're going to let us hold the election?"

"Following certain rules and conditions," he said.

I hated conditions and I wasn't so good at following rules. "What?"

"Perhaps other people think the school team should remain the Laggan Lairds. It must be allowed to be on the ballot. Is that agreeable?"

"Sure, of course, no problem, sir," Sarah said.

"And you must establish rules that follow the common practices of democratic elections," he said.

"What does that mean?" I asked.

"Polling booths, secret ballots, limited

election campaigns and no threats or bribes."

"I don't think anybody is going to be threatening people," I said.

"Good, then there won't be any difficulties following those rules."

"I have one more question," I said.

"Yes?"

"I want to know that whatever name is officially elected by the majority of voters will become the name of the school teams. I don't want to go to all this work if it's just going to stay the Lairds."

Mr. McGregor stood up and reached out his hand. "You have my word." We shook on it.

chapter five

"The first thing we have to discuss is how nominating a name is different than nominating a person," Mr. Davidson said.

"How is it different?" Sarah asked.

"For one thing, when you nominate a person that person is able to launch a campaign and tell you why they should be elected. Who will speak up for a nominated name?" he asked.

"How about the person who suggests that name," Tanner suggested.

"That sounds right to me. If somebody thinks a name is a good one they should be willing to campaign for that name," Taylor agreed.

"But what if somebody has an idea—an idea that is really good—but they don't want to campaign for it?" Kelsey asked.

"I think if somebody else is willing to take on the name and be its champion then that's okay."

"And if nobody is willing?" I asked.

"Then the name can't be nominated," Mr. Davidson said.

"Does it have to be just one person or could it be more than one who works with a name?" Sarah asked.

"You mean like a delegation?" I asked sarcastically.

Before she could answer back, Mr. Davidson spoke. "I think each name could have a whole committee of people. I think since this is a class project, every member of the class should be on a campaign."

That sounded like work. It was too late in the year for work, but I wasn't in a position to object since I'd started the ball rolling in the first place.

"I'm still not sure about the kindergarten kids voting," Tanner said.

"Because they're too young?" Mr. Davidson asked.

"Because they're too stupid," he answered.

"No name-calling," Mr. Davidson warned. "I think that should be one of the ground rules for the entire campaign. No name-calling. You're allowed to say why your name is better but not why another name is worse."

"Isn't that sort of the same thing?" Sarah asked.

"Not quite. Saying Laggan is a good school filled with wonderful students is much different than telling everybody that Maple Ridge is a bad school with bad kids."

"Maybe different, but generally true," I said and people began laughing.

"You really have a thing for that school, don't you?" Mr. Davidson said.

"If you think hate is a thing then you're right," I agreed.

Mr. Davidson took a deep breath before continuing. "We need somebody to write down the rules."

"I will!" Sarah exclaimed.

Big shock, big surprise, big suck-up.

"To start, each name must be nominated by one person and be seconded—that means agreed to by one other person. Each nominated name must have a champion, one person who acts as its campaign manager."

"And it can be more than just one person, right?" Sarah asked.

"It can be up to ten people. Elections will take place in two weeks, secret ballot, and there will be no attempts to buy, bribe or threaten voters to influence them to vote for your choice of name. And, finally, no negative advertisement. You can only say what's right with your name but say nothing negative about another. Those are the rules."

"I've got them," Sarah said.

"Good. Can you please read them back to me, just to be sure."

Sarah started to recite the rules. When Mr. Davidson had listed them, they'd all seemed reasonable. Coming out of Sarah's mouth they sounded bossy.

"Thank you. Now, all in favor of the rules raise your hand."

Hands shot up around the room.

"Opposed?" Mr. Davidson asked.

No hands.

"The rules are approved in a true democratic fashion. Let me now open up the floor for nominations."

Hands flew up and names were added to the list on the chalkboard. The first three names that were proposed, and seconded, were names you'd expect: Lions, Leopards and Lynx. Apparently there were lots of members of the cat family that had names that started with *l*.

"Does it have to start with an *l*?" Tanner asked.

"I don't think it has to start with anything.

It's just tradition that there is often alliteration in team names," Mr. Davidson said.

"What's alliteration?" Kelsey asked.

"It means things all starting with the same letter of the alphabet. It's common practice. Did you have something in mind, Tanner?"

"I was thinking the Lizards," he answered.

"But Lizards does start with *l*, that is alliteration."

"I know," he said. "I just wanted to know if I could do it a different way."

"How about the Laggan Dragons?" Cody asked.

"Certainly. I like the sound of that," Mr. Davidson said. "Any other suggestions?"

"Leprechauns," Sarah said.

"What?" I asked in stunned response.

"Leprechauns. They're magical and mythical and—"

"And green and tiny," I said cutting her off. "What would the players get at half time? Lucky Charms instead of oranges and Gatorade?"

"Would our team be magically delicious?" Tanner questioned.

"How about if teams beat us they get a pot of gold or maybe—"

"I think that's enough," Mr. Davidson said, ending the discussion. "There will be no negative campaigning even when we're choosing the names."

"So do you want to campaign for your little suggestion?" I asked Sarah.

"Well..."

"I didn't think so. Anybody else?" I asked the class. Nobody volunteered. "That settles it, lets go back to *real* names."

"Leprechaun is real," Sarah said, defending what she really didn't want to defend.

"It's as real as leprechauns. Doesn't exist, just made up."

"He's right, Sarah," Tanner said. "If you're going to nominate that name you might as well call us the Laggan Lard Butts."

"That's disgusting!" Sarah said, turning up her nose.

"It's not disgusting," I disagreed. "The proper way to say Laird is lard, so maybe Lard Butts makes more sense than Leprechauns."

"Mr. Davidson, you can't let them suggest that name," Sarah pleaded.

"So far it hasn't been nominated. We haven't had a formal nomination or a second," he said.

"I'll nominate it!" Tanner called out. "I think the school teams should go by the name Laggan Lard Butts. Do I have somebody to second my nomination?"

"I second it!" Taylor yelled out.

"Sir, they can't really put that name forward, can they?" Sarah asked.

Before he could answer I jumped in. "According to the rules there's no reason why they can't. It doesn't break any of the rules, does it Mr. Davidson?"

"Not break, but it hasn't satisfied all the rules yet. So far we have a name but nobody to campaign for it."

"That's right!" Sarah exclaimed. "So, Sam, will you be the campaign chairman for the Lard Butts?"

"I didn't suggest it."

"Lots of talk, but nothing to back it up," Sarah taunted.

"Fine, I'll do it," I said before I'd had time to think about what I was saying. "I'm going to be the chair and I need people to work with me."

"Count me in," Tanner said.

"I'm in too!" Taylor yelled out.

"Then that makes it official. Any more names to add to the mix?" Mr. Davidson asked.

"Not another name," Sarah said. "I was just hoping that there was space on the Leopard team for me to be part of it."

"Sure!" Katie exclaimed. "I'm glad you can help me."

Sarah smiled at Katie and then looked at me. "I'm happy to try to change the name to something good."

I smiled back. Let the games begin.

chapter six

I put up a shot. It hit the rim and bounced away. I'd hardly made a shot during the whole warm-up. I hoped that old saying was true: bad warm-up, great game.

"So any ideas?" Tanner asked.

"Let's start zone and then go man if they start hitting from the outside."

"I'm not talking about the game. I meant do you have ideas about the campaign?"

"What?" I asked in disbelief.

"The campaign, the name change. Do you have any ideas? I've been thinking we really have an uphill battle to get people to choose Lard Butts as a team name."

"How about if we talk about the *team* instead of the team *name*," I suggested.

"We really have to talk about this."

"Now?" I asked, gesturing around me.

"I guess it can wait until after the game," he said.

"If we don't win this game we'll have lots of time because that will be the end of our season," Taylor added.

I hated the thought of losing, but winning didn't have much appeal either. If we won we'd get into the play-offs. Getting into the play-offs meant playing the first place team—the team that had killed us in the two games we'd played, the team that would kill us again in the play-offs. Maybe it would be better to have a close loss to end the season now instead of a blowout embarrassment later.

"Think we can take 'em?" Taylor asked.

They're not that much better than us. We could have taken them that first game."

"Could have, should have, would have, didn't," I said.

"Just think," Tanner said. "If we beat them our reward is getting killed in the play-offs. It might be easier to end it all here."

"Don't say that!" I snapped angrily.

"I don't mean we should try to lose!" he said, defending himself.

"I know, I know." I hadn't been angry with him as much as I was mad at myself for thinking what he'd had the guts to say.

"What happens afterward doesn't matter. What happens now does. We're gonna take these guys."

"Time-out!" Taylor yelled as he fell on the loose ball and wrapped his arms around it.

The ref whistled down the player. Tanner offered his brother a hand and pulled him to his feet.

"Way to go buddy, way to go!" Cody exclaimed.

I looked up at the clock. We were up by

one point with seven seconds left on the clock and we had the ball! It would be pretty hard to lose now. We'd won our third win of the year and—wait a second—they had three wins too. Who would finish sixth?

"Coach, what happens when two teams are tied at the end of the season?"

"What?" Mr. Davidson asked.

"Tiebreakers. What happens if two teams are tied at the end of the season? Who gets sixth place?"

"I'm not really sure. Probably head to head games."

"But we both will have won once," Taylor said.

"Then possibly total score in those games."

Instantly I knew. They'd beaten us by two points in the first game. If we only beat them by one point, then they'd take sixth, and we'd be out of the play-offs. For a fraction of a second I had to fight a sense of relief.

"We have to score. We have to beat them by more than two points or they're in and we're out," I said.

"Are you sure?" Tanner asked.

"I'm not sure about anything. Do you have a copy of the tiebreaker rules in your shorts? I just know we have to try to score. Winning isn't enough." I looked at Mr. Davidson. "Coach?"

"Go for it."

"Okay. Tanner you throw the ball in. Everybody else get in tight. I'm going to break long so you have to heave a football pass to me. Got it?"

"Piece of cake."

"Okay, let's break and—"

"Wait," Tanner said. "Everybody put your hands together."

Hand over hand we piled our hands making a big, multi-layered hand sandwich.

"On three I want everybody to yell, *Go, Lard Butts!*"

We all looked at him with the same stunned expression.

The score table buzzed to signal the end of the time-out.

"You heard me. I want you all to give that cheer."

"Is that okay, Coach?" Cody asked.

"Why not?"

"Good," Tanner said. "One, two, three—"

"Go, Lard Butts!" we all yelled and then we burst into laughter.

Suddenly all of the tension was gone. Everybody looked relaxed. We got into position on the court.

The ref handed the ball to Tanner. We settled into a tight stack, and the crowd began cheering for their team to take away the ball and score. I broke quickly in and then cut back in the opposite direction. I was completely open, and Tanner tossed the ball. It was long and way over my head! I jumped up, extending as far as I could. The ball just brushed the tips of my fingers. I chased it down, grabbed the ball and went for a lay-up. The ball dropped through the net at the same time the buzzer sounded. It counted!

We'd won, and, even better, we were in the play-offs!

chapter seven

We all stood at attention in the office while
the last few notes of the national anthem
played. Over to the side, beside their
mailboxes, a couple of teachers were holding
a whispered conversation. I fought the urge
to shush them the way they would have if
it had been us talking. Did respect for your
country stop when you got to a certain age
and position? I was pretty darn proud of

myself for not saying anything, though. At the start of the school year I would have, but now I was starting to understand that it would only get me in trouble.

"Please be seated," Taylor said over the PA as the music ended.

Students worked in threes to do the announcements each week. It was our week. Personally I hated it, but both Tanner and Taylor were hams. They would have liked to be in charge of the announcements every week.

"The senior choir will meet at first recess in the music room to rehearse for the graduation assembly," Tanner said.

He handed me the microphone.

"This is the last week to hand in permission forms for the grade eight field trip," I read off the sheet. "Remember, no form, no trip."

I made a mental note. I hadn't returned my form yet. I was pretty sure it was somewhere in my locker, or my bedroom, or maybe my backpack. That narrowed it down.

"Now for our thought of the day, as written by our principal, Mr. McGregor.

'Winners never quit and quitters never win,'"
Taylor read. "Definitely words to live by. And
speaking of winning, yesterday, in a dramatic
win, the boys' senior basketball team won
their game by a score of forty-three to forty.
This win propelled the team into sixth place
in the standings and into the play-offs. The
first play-off game is scheduled for next
Tuesday."

Tanner came up and took the microphone
and both he and his brother leaned right into
it. "Go, Lard Butts!" they yelled.

My mouth dropped open. I looked over.
The two teachers by the mailboxes had
stopped talking.

"And that concludes our morning
announcements. Have a great day!" Tanner
sang out and then put the microphone down
on the top of the file cabinet.

We started to walk out of the office.

"How'd you like our little advertisement?"
Tanner asked.

"Caught me by surprise," I admitted.

"We need name brand recognition,"
Taylor said.

"What?"

He chuckled. "I was reading about advertising on the Internet last night. The secret to selling something is to get everybody talking about it."

"But we're not selling anything," I argued.

"Yes we are. We're selling a name."

"And the only way to get people to buy that name is for everybody to see and hear it everywhere. We have to make banners and posters and—"

He stopped mid-sentence and we all skidded to a stop. There on the wall was a poster. In big bold letters it read, *Leap forward and vote for the Laggan Leopards*.

"I think somebody else checked out the Internet last night," I said.

"I think somebody named Sarah," Tanner said, "at least judging from the art work on that poster." There was a beautifully drawn picture of a leopard leaping through the air. Sarah wasn't just the student president, she wasn't just really smart, she was also the best artist in the school. She was really annoying.

"What do we draw on our posters?" Taylor asked.

"That's a problem. It's isn't like we can draw a really fat—"

"Shouldn't you boys be getting to class?"

We spun around. It was Mr. McGregor. He didn't look too happy...then again, did he ever really look happy?

"Interesting announcements this morning," he said, cutting off my thought.

"We try to do a good job," Tanner said. "By the way, your thought of the day was one of your best."

"Really got me thinking," Taylor agreed.

Mr. McGregor looked even less happy. "Would one of you like to explain that last part of the announcements?"

Tanner and Taylor looked at each other as if they had no idea what he was talking about. I wondered if they were trying to make me explain. I wasn't that stupid.

"Oh, do you mean the 'Go, Lard Butts' part?" Tanner asked, trying to sound innocent.

Mr. McGregor nodded sternly.

"I guess that was a little out of line, but we're just so excited about the contest you gave permission for...you know, renaming the school teams."

"You want to call the school team the Lard Butts?" he asked in shock.

"That's one of the nominated names," Tanner said. "Not quite as catchy as Leopards, is it?" he said pointing at the poster. "Leap forward and vote for the Laggan Leopards," he said. "That is one catchy slogan."

I knew what they were doing. They were trying to distract him. They were very good at that.

"Probably the winning slogan," Taylor added. "Can't see any other winning."

"I don't know," Tanner said. "The Laggan Dragons is pretty good too, but I have to wait to hear their slogan."

"Probably something about catch fire for the Laggan Dragons, you know because of fire-breathing dragons. It's even medieval like the Lairds so it sort of has tradition on its side."

"Who, may I dare ask, suggested the name

Lard Butts?" Mr. McGregor asked. So much for distraction.

"Originally?" Tanner asked.

"Yes."

"Well, I'm not really sure, I wasn't there. It was somebody from another school. Do you remember who it was, Sam?" Taylor asked.

"Me?"

"Yeah, well it was you who he said it to."

"Um, the point guard, the backup point guard, for Maple Ridge, number four, but I don't know his name."

"And I imagine it was you who then suggested it for the school team name," Mr. McGregor said.

"No, not me!" I said, holding up my hands.

"Then who?" he asked, his gaze shifting back and forth between the twins.

"I think it was me," Tanner said.

"It might have been me," Taylor said. "It's funny, even we get confused which one of us is which."

I burst out laughing, but Mr. McGregor's fierce look burned that out really quickly.

"Do you boys really believe that Lard Butts is an appropriate name for the school team?"

Neither twin answered. Both of them looked down at their feet.

"Well, boys, do you?"

"I guess not really," Taylor said, still not looking up at Mr. McGregor.

"Maybe not the best," Tanner agreed.

"Good, because I'm going to disallow that name."

"I don't think you can," I said.

Now everybody's mouths dropped open.

"What did you say?" Mr. McGregor asked.

"I don't think you can. Lard Butts isn't a bad word. It was nominated by one person and seconded by another. According to the rules—the rules you approved—there's nothing wrong with it."

"It is disrespectful."

"Maybe it is and maybe it isn't. That isn't the question. I just don't think you can simply wave your hand and make that name go away."

"No one is waving his hand, but I am the principal."

"That's why you can't do it," I said. "You gave your word that we could nominate names. You set the rules and now you want to change them. What sort of message is that? That if you're in charge you don't have to keep your word? Is that how it works in a democracy? If you don't like one of the candidates you simply say they can't run?"

"Well, no," Mr. McGregor reluctantly agreed.

"Then I don't think you should try to do that here. Besides, nobody is actually going to vote for Lard Butts—maybe three people will—so what is it going to hurt?"

Mr. McGregor didn't answer right away. That was probably a good thing.

"I gave my word and I will not break it. Let the best name win," Mr. McGregor said.

"Thanks, sir," Tanner gushed.

"Now you should get to class."

Mr. McGregor walked off in one direction and we continued to move the opposite way.

"That was the bravest thing I ever saw in my whole life," Tanner said.

"Not that brave."

"You're like my hero," Taylor agreed.

"Big deal. It doesn't mean anything. Now we just get to spend more time trying to get people to vote for something that has no chance of winning."

"No chance?" Tanner demanded.

"Yes, no chance."

"I don't believe my ears," Taylor said. "Didn't you listen to the announcements today? A quitter never wins and a Lard Butt never quits. Go, Lard Butts!"

chapter eight

Mr. Davidson had basically suspended all classes in language arts. Instead of the usual grammar and novel study, we were working on our election campaigns. Every single person in the class was on one campaign or another.

Some of the things the other groups were coming up with were really good, really creative. Big beautiful banners and posters lined the halls and the front entrance. One group had written a song. It wasn't a great song—it was called "The Lions Never Lie Down"—but still it was a song.

Mr. Davidson had also assigned each group to come up with a cheer. We hadn't finished ours. Actually we hadn't started it yet.

"Okay, I've got some ideas for the motto," Tanner said. "Ready?"

"Breathless."

"The Laggan Lard Butts, feel the power."

I giggled. "I'm not sure anything to do with feeling butts is such a good thing."

"Good point. I hadn't thought about that. Okay, here's my second one. Laggan Lard Butts, smell the victory."

This time both Taylor and I burst into laughter.

"What's so funny?" Tanner demanded.

"I think smelling butts is probably worse than feeling them," I explained.

Tanner smiled. "I guess that suggestion sort of stinks, which is appropriate for Butts.

Okay, my last suggestion. The Laggan Lard Butts—Why not?"

"Why not?" I questioned.

"Yeah, don't you think it's catchy?"

"I think it's *something*," I admitted.

"Look, Sam, everybody else has something cute. It's hard to come up with something catchy for Lard Butts—as you've pointed out with my last two suggestions—so this makes sense. Why not vote for it is a question people need to think through. We want them to think about this name as a possibility."

"Getting them thinking could work against us. Anybody who thinks will know there are better choices."

"Keep your voice down," Taylor cautioned me. "We can't afford to have somebody overhear you putting down your own name."

That made sense. "If you weren't voting for our name, what name would you vote for?" I asked.

"That's a hard one," Tanner said.

"There are lots of good choices," Taylor agreed.

"So which one is the best choice?" I asked.

"Maybe the Lions," Tanner said. "Lions are tough, and they've done a great job with their campaign."

"The Lynx might be my choice," Taylor added. "You know it's a cat, but it's a small cat, just like we're a small school. And there are lynx around here."

"There are?" I asked.

"Well, I don't know about *right* around here. I've never seen one, but they are native to this area."

"If I was running that campaign I'd make sure people knew about that," Tanner said. "What about you, Sam?"

"I think I would go with Laggan Dragons because it's different. Besides, a dragon is a mythical creature that doesn't exist and we have a nonexistent chance of winning that play-off game."

Tanner stood up and put a hand on my shoulder. "Samuel," he said, trying to sound very adult, "how many times must I remind you that a Lard Butt doesn't quit?"

"Wait, maybe that should be our motto!" Taylor exclaimed. "A Lard Butt doesn't quit!"

"I like it. Sammy?"

"Sure beats any of the other suggestions. Let's put that on our new posters. How are our new posters doing?" I asked.

"Do you want fast or do you want right?" Tanner asked.

"I'd settle for either. When will they be up?"

"I'll bring them tomorrow. You seem to be in a big rush, for somebody who doesn't think we have a chance."

"I don't, but that doesn't mean I'm not going to try."

"You hear what the Leopards are doing?" Taylor asked.

"What?" I asked, although it would probably be better if I didn't know.

"You know how Sarah helps with the kindergartens at morning recess?" Taylor said.

"Yeah."

"She's been down there telling them that

she's with the Leopard team and that they should all vote for the Leopards."

"That doesn't surprise me."

"She's even been giving them little Leopard stickers," Tanner added.

"She can't do that."

"She's already doing it."

"No, she can't, she can't do that!" I exclaimed.

I jumped to my feet and the twins jumped up after me. I rushed over to Mr. Davidson.

"Mr. Davidson, one of the teams is cheating!" I said in a very loud voice.

He looked up from his desk. Suddenly the sound of people working faded. Nobody in the room was working anymore; they were all watching me.

"One of the teams is cheating," I repeated.

"Those are pretty strong words. Please explain."

"Isn't it illegal and anti-democratic to buy votes?" I asked.

"Of course. And you think one of the teams is buying votes?"

"Not think. *Know*." I turned around and pointed directly at the Leopards' table. "The Leopards are giving stickers to the kindergartens!"

There were actually gasps from people. It felt like a court drama in the movies.

"Is this true, Sarah?" he asked.

"We're giving them stickers, but not in exchange for their votes."

"Then why are you giving them leopard stickers?" I demanded.

"I'm giving them stickers so they'll vote for Leopards," she said.

"So you admit it!"

"But I'm not buying their votes. I'm just trying to influence them to vote for Leopards."

"I don't really see the difference and if I can't understand it I don't think those kindergarten kids can either."

"You're probably not as smart as those little kids in kinder—"

"Mr. Davidson!" Tanner yelled out. "It sounds like she's going to put somebody down. It's bad enough they're trying to buy votes. Now they have started insulting people."

"But...but..."

"It's *Lard* Butt, not but, but," Tanner said, cutting her off again.

"Well, Mr. Davidson, is Sarah allowed to give things to voters or not?" I asked.

He looked at me, then at Sarah, and back at me. He shook his head. "No giveaways."

Tanner and Taylor began to cheer. So did more than half the class.

Maybe Lard Butts wasn't going to win. But at least we'd make it hard for the Leopards to succeed.

chapter nine

"Could Samuel, Taylor and Tanner please report to the office," Mr. McGregor called out over the PA.

We looked at each other. The rest of the lunchroom stopped eating and looked at us too.

"But we haven't done anything wrong, have we?" Taylor asked.

"Nothing that anybody knows about," Tanner added.

"He didn't sound angry," Taylor said.

"He never sounds angry," I said.

"What do you think he wants?"

"Only one way to find out. Come on."

We gathered up the remains of our lunches. I always tried to act cool about being in the office, but I never had an appetite after a trip down there. Even after all the times I'd been sent to the office, it still bothered me. I tossed my lunch in the garbage can—basket!

We shuffled down the hall and into the office. The secretary was away at lunch. Behind the counter were two students, Katie and Sarah. I had to fight the urge to turn around and leave. I'd forgotten Sarah did this during lunch sometimes.

Sarah looked up from the desk and smiled at us—no smile wasn't the right word. She smirked. How could I ever have liked that girl? How could I ever have gone out with her? What an idiot I was!

"What a surprise, the three of you are in the office and in trouble," she said sweetly.

"What a surprise, you're in the office being a suck-up," I replied, equally as sweetly.

The smirk vanished and she turned red in the face. I always could make her turn red, either in embarrassment or frustration.

"That was really unfair, bringing up those stickers," Sarah said.

"The only unfair thing was giving them away to begin with."

"I wasn't doing anything wrong!" she protested.

"I guess that was why Mr. Davidson made you stop, because you were doing nothing wrong. Don't get mad at me for simply pointing out what you were doing."

Before she could answer, Mr. McGregor poked his head out of his office. He gestured for us to come in. Taylor and Tanner went inside right away. I took a side trip, grabbed a chair and carried it into his office with me. They were already seated when I brought the chair in. I put it down beside Taylor—no, Tanner.

"Sam could you please close the door," Mr. McGregor asked.

"Yeah, sure." I turned around and closed it. This was not a good sign.

"I don't like my conversations to be overheard," he explained.

I sat down. At that same instant Mr. McGregor got up from his seat, circled his desk and perched on its edge. This was different. Different made me nervous.

"So, boys, how is the campaign going?" he asked.

Was he snarling? No that was a smile.

I waited for one of the twins to answer. They were waiting for me. I guess it was best to go with experience. I had the most experience with office visits so it was up to me.

"It's going pretty good."

"There were some great suggestions," he said. "I have my personal favorite, although it's best that I don't tell anybody. I wouldn't want to influence the students by telling them which one I want to win."

I was pretty sure Lard Butts wasn't on his shortlist.

"I'm more interested in how *your* campaign is going." He gave that same snarly sort of smile. I felt like shuddering. I liked his serious yelling face much better.

"Okay, I guess."

"Not as good as some of them," Tanner chipped in, again trying to move the conversation in a different direction. That was smart.

"Some of the teams have fancy posters and banners and cheers," he said.

"We don't even have a motto really," Taylor said.

"Yeah, I think we're in last place," Tanner said.

Mr. McGregor's face seemed to loosen up a little. I'm sure that made him happy.

"I was wondering if you boys could do me a favor," he said.

"Sure!" Tanner said.

"Of course," Taylor agreed.

"Depends on the favor," I said, and all three of them looked at me. The sound of escaping air came from Mr. McGregor.

"I wonder if you would consider—and this is strictly your choice, you are under no pressure whatsoever—allowing the name Lard Butt to be removed from the list?"

"It's not going to win," I said.

"Hopefully not."

I laughed. "So much for not telling us what name you want to win."

"I didn't tell you what I want to win," he said. "I'm telling you what name I *don't* want to win."

"Don't worry, it won't win. Like I said, it's in third or fourth place at best."

"It is now." He paused. "You three have a great deal of influence with your peers."

"We do?" I asked.

"Certainly. You're popular and play on all the teams. Winning your last game certainly didn't hurt. And even when you *occasionally* get into trouble it's not for doing anything hurtful toward another student."

"Never."

"Generally you're friends with, and friendly to, almost everybody," he said.

"Almost everybody." He'd probably heard me bickering with Sarah. There was something about her that brought out the worst in me. That smug little smile, always knowing the answers, how she always had her makeup done just perfectly, wore the right clothes and smelled so good and—

"So would you consider abandoning your campaign?" he asked.

Tanner and Taylor both looked over at me, as if it was my decision.

"I don't think we can do that," I said. "A winner never quits and a quitter never wins, right?"

He nodded his head slowly. "I didn't think you'd agree, but I felt obligated to ask. Thanks for listening. Please go and finish your lunch."

"Thanks."

We all got up. We started to leave and I remembered I'd brought a chair into the office. I bumped past the twins to grab it.

"I really don't think it's going to win," I said to Mr. McGregor.

"I think you might be right, but you could be wrong. Do you really want the teams to be called the Lard Butts?"

I shrugged.

"Keep that in mind as you continue your campaign."

chapter ten

I looked down at the empty end of the court. There was only five minutes left until the start of the game, and the Traynor Tigers hadn't even come out for their warm-up. They hadn't been delayed in traffic. It was their home game, in their gym, at their school. I didn't think they were in their change room, desperately planning a way to beat us. All they had to do was walk out onto the court to do that.

"Where are they?" Tanner asked.

I shrugged. "Want me to go into their dressing room and check?"

"Aren't they going to warm up at all?" Taylor asked.

"Maybe they figure they don't need to warm up to beat us," I suggested.

"I'd be insulted if we didn't resemble that remark."

"We could surprise them," Taylor said.

"For us to win we'd have to go beyond surprise, past shock and halfway to a miracle," I said.

"So you *do* think we have a chance. Miracles *do* happen," Taylor said.

"A win would be really good for our campaign. If we can keep winning then we could give the Lard Butt cheer more exposure," Tanner said.

"You sure you want Butts exposed?" I asked.

"You know what I mean. Can you imagine how kids would vote if we won the championship?"

"I'm just trying to imagine how this crowd would react if we won today," I said, gesturing to the bleachers. There wasn't an empty seat. There had to be at least two hundred people here to watch the Tigers devour the Lairds.

"How come we never get crowds like that for our home games?" Tanner asked.

"First, we don't have that many kids in our whole school," I said. "And second, since we're a bus school most of them are gone before our games even start."

"That makes sense. But wouldn't it be great to have a big crowd cheering for us?"

"It would be great if we could do something that they'd want to cheer about. This crowd isn't here to see a basketball game."

"They're not?"

"No. They're here to see a basketball victory. They came because they want to see their team win, or, even better, blow us out. They came to see their team destroy us."

"Can you imagine how they'd react if we won?" Tanner asked.

"I can't imagine, but I'd love to see it." I paused. "And, who knows, things happen."

"Then you do believe it's possible!" Tanner exclaimed. "You do believe in miracles!"

"I'd believe in them more if we had a center. Why couldn't you two have been one really tall baby instead of twins?"

"Talk to our mother."

Suddenly the crowd started to roar. Their team was finally coming out of the dressing room. The players went over to their bench, put down their gear and started a brief warm-up. The clock showed less than two minutes to the start of the game.

"We better warm up again as well," I said.

I dribbled to the three-point line and put up a shot. It went straight in!

"Save a few of those for the game when we'll need them," Tanner said.

"We'll need more than a few of those. We won't be scoring much from the inside against their big man."

Mr. Davidson called us over to the bench, and we gathered around him.

"Usual starters," he said.

That was about the only direction he ever gave us at the beginning of a game.

"What defense should we start with?" he asked.

"We have to stop their center. Everything goes through him," I said. "Zone, pack it down low, try to keep him from getting easy looks."

"He makes them all look easy," Taylor said.

Their center was probably the best player in the whole league. He was definitely the tallest. He scored half of their points every game. I would have loved to see how they'd play without him.

"Cody can you make him pay for his points?" I asked. "In hockey what would you do if a forward kept coming into your crease when you're in net?"

Cody smiled. "I'd take my goalie stick and give him a good whack on the back of his legs, cut him down like firewood."

"Okay," I said, slowly shaking my head. I made a mental note to never go into the crease when he was playing net. "Maybe that won't work here, but try to push him around a little anyway."

"I'll do my best."

"And don't forget that we're not going to get the tip. Forwards, you have to jump into the spots you think their center is going to direct the ball to. Guards, you drop back to defend. Okay, let's break and—"

"Before we do that I just want to say something," Mr. Davidson said. "I know I don't know much about basketball, but I do know about kids. I have been so honored to be able to—"

"Hold on there, Coach," Tanner said, cutting him off. "You can't give that speech until the last game of the season. Maybe this won't be our last game."

"Possibly it is."

"Possibly it isn't. Remember we haven't lost one single game since we started to use the new cheer. Some people believe in miracles," he said, winking at me. "Other people believe in luck. Everybody put your hands in."

We formed a pile.

"On three, Go, Lard Butts. One, two, three."

We screamed our cheer and then five of us trotted toward center court and—what was going on here? Their center wasn't on the court. I looked over at their bench. He was sitting at the end, his head in his hands. On the bench beside him were the usual starting point guard and one of their forwards. They were starting their subs! They thought so little of us that they thought they could beat us with their second stringers!

I felt myself start to get red. I felt the anger building up inside and—no, I wasn't going to let it make me crazy.

"Wait!" I yelled out. "Everybody here!"

The four other starters gathered around me.

"I want a full-court press with man to man defense. Cody, you go up for the tip. Smash the ball as hard as you can toward their basket. I'll go and get it. Now break."

We tapped hands with each of their players. A little courtesy before the game was always nice, even when you didn't feel any.

Cody lined up beside their center. Cody was a shade taller and thicker. He wouldn't be able to jump as high as their center, but he might be able to overpower him. The ref tossed the ball up, and I turned and ran for their net. The ball soared over my head and past me! I raced after it, grabbing it before it bounced out of bounds. I turned around just in time to see Taylor streaking toward the net. I fired in a pass. He put it up and scored! We had the lead. It might be our only lead of the game but we'd scored first.

"Press! Press! Press!" I screamed.

Everybody locked on his man. The ball was passed in, bounced off the fingertips of one of their players and right to Tanner. He dribbled in, uncovered, and put up our second basket!

"Press!" I yelled.

The pass came in, and Taylor and Cody trapped the ball carrier in the corner. He made a wild pass. I grabbed it, stopped, turned and fired up an equally wild three-point shot. It dropped! We were up seven to nothing!

I looked over at their bench to give them a smirk. Their centre got to his feet. I thought that was the end of our winning streak; he was coming in. He walked over to the score table—no *past* the score table. He walked over to the far corner of the gym, bent over and threw up in the big plastic garbage can!

"Sam, do we keep on the press?" Taylor asked.

I was startled out of my thoughts. "Yeah, keep pressing, keep pressing!"

By the time the game was half over, it was really over. The players on their team, who weren't running to the washroom to throw up, were sitting on the bench too sick and too weak to play. Half the team—and most of the starters—had been hit with the flu bug! They must have felt awful, in more ways than one. I almost felt sorry for them. Almost. I thought about how much pity they'd shown us in the two blowout victories they'd had.

Go, Lard Butts, Go!

chapter eleven

"Lard Butts?"

I looked up from my desk to see my father standing at my bedroom door.

"How did you hear?"

"I got a call from Mr. McGregor."

"I can't believe he called you."

"Why not? Our home phone number must be on his speed dial," my father said.

"Not lately."

"Come to think of it, it has been a

while," my father agreed. "Does that mean you've been staying out of trouble, or you're not getting caught? Or has Mr. McGregor given up because you're leaving soon?"

I laughed. "Maybe a little of all of the above. So what did he say?"

"He told me about the contest to rename the teams. I always thought Lairds was a pretty stupid name. I think everybody always thought that. Finally one person was brave enough—or stupid enough—to suggest it." He pointed at me.

"I fit one of those categories."

"Sometimes you fit both. Couldn't you come up with a better name than Lard Butts?" he asked.

"There are lots of other names. Lizards, Dragons, Lynx, Leopards, Lions—"

"Leopards, now that's a name for a team. I wouldn't have minded being a Laggan Leopard when I played for the school."

"That's my least favorite of all. I'd rather be a Lard Butt."

"Wouldn't it be better to be a Lion or a Dragon instead of a Lard Butt?"

"Maybe. Probably. Yes."

"Then why are you trying to change the name to Lard Butts?"

I shrugged. "It just sort of happened."

"And now that it's just sort of happened, you don't know how to stop it, right?"

I shook my head. "But that's okay. It's not like it's going to actually win."

"Mr. McGregor thinks it might."

"He said that?" I asked in amazement.

"He didn't say that, but if he wasn't worried he wouldn't have called."

I hadn't really thought of that. Why would he be wasting his time on a name that didn't have a chance? That thought made me happy and nervous at the same time.

"What exactly did he say?"

"He didn't say it in so many words, but I think he was hoping that I could convince you to rethink this."

"And you said?"

"I said that it's rare enough that you *think*, so having you *re*think might be asking too much," he said and started to laugh.

"No, seriously, what did you say?"

"Nothing. I just listened."

I waited for my father to go on, but he didn't.

"Do you think we should rethink it?" I asked.

"I know that most of what gets you in trouble is that you're too stubborn to admit when you're wrong. In this case, you won't change your mind even though you know you're wrong."

"I'm not necessarily wrong. It's just a name. They can always hold another election next year if they don't like the name that wins this year."

"I guess you have a point," he said. "But if you combed your hair—"

"A different way it wouldn't show," I said, finishing his very bad, very old joke.

"Yeah. You know me, I'm not going to tell you what to do."

"Especially about being too stubborn. No question which parent I get that from," I said.

"Let's not say bad things about your mother. I'm just saying it would be okay if you changed your mind."

"I know. So what did you think about the result of today's play-off game?"

"That's right, you had a game today. Who won?"

"Mr. McGregor didn't tell you that when he called?" I asked in amazement.

"No. What happened?"

"We won! We beat the first place team!"

"Way to go. So what happens now?"

"The way the play-offs are scheduled the first place team, or the team that plays them and wins—like us, gets a spot in the finals. The other teams have to win their first game and then the winners have a second play-off game to get to the finals against us. The final is this Thursday, and it's a home game for us!"

"That is incredible. You must be so excited. You have a chance to win the whole thing in front of your home crowd."

"Not much of a chance."

"There are only going to be two teams there, so you have the same chance as them."

"Not really. Out of six teams that made the play-offs we finished sixth."

"Didn't you just tell me that you beat the first place team?" my father asked.

"They were short a player or two," I said—although it was more like five or six.

"How did you do against the other teams during the regular season?"

"We lost both games."

"Close losses?"

"If you consider twenty-five points close, then, some of them barely squeaked by us."

My father laughed.

"All I know is that I'm going to be in the gym cheering your team on." He paused. "I could even make a sign."

"That's okay," I said, thinking about what embarrassing thing he might put on a sign. "What are you going to put on the sign?"

"Something simple...maybe just three words...Go Lard Butts!"

chapter twelve

"Are you nervous?" Tanner asked.

"A bit. You?"

"Nothing to be nervous about."

I wasn't sure about that. We were sitting on stage along with two representatives from the five other nominated names. The whole school—every kid, every teacher, even the janitor—were in the gym. Each group had two minutes to speak about their name. Mr. McGregor was going speak about keeping the name Laird. Nobody had campaigned for it, but, as he'd said in the beginning, people had the right to vote for it. I had to hand it to him. He really didn't want Lard Butts to be selected, but he kept his word.

After the speeches the gym would be converted into a polling station. Mr. Davidson had printed official ballots. We had ballot boxes, and the secretary was the polling officer. The janitor and two parents had agreed to count the votes. I was glad it wasn't Mr. McGregor. I knew he wouldn't cheat, but the fact that the thought even crossed my mind made me nervous.

There had been a draw to determine the order of the presentations. We'd drawn last place. Tanner said that was good because we got the final word. I thought it was bad because we got to stay nervous for the whole thing. Everybody else got to speak and then they could sit down and relax.

Mr. McGregor walked to the microphone at the front of the stage. He raised his hand to signal for silence. Slowly the entire crowd, including the teachers, raised their hands and went silent. I kept my arms folded across my chest.

"Good morning, students."

"Good morning, Mr. McGregor!" the crowd bellowed back.

"We are here today to practice something very important: democracy. One student, one vote, all of us equal, will decide."

People started cheering and clapping.

"Your right to vote comes with a responsibility. You must choose wisely. Do not *waste* your vote."

I felt my cheeks burning. Was it my imagination or was everybody looking at me and Tanner?

"We will now start with the first presentation. Please welcome Heather and Brian."

The crowd gave a polite round of applause, and the two of them walked to the podium. They talked about why everybody should vote for Lynx as the name of the school team. They said that the lynx was native to the area and was powerful and small—small like our school.

That sounded like a pretty good argument. It also sounded familiar. Hadn't Taylor said those same things? I looked at him in the audience. He shrugged and gave a little smile. He hadn't been able to resist telling them his ideas.

They finished by holding up a big banner with a picture of a lynx. It was in shades of black and orange. Very nice artwork. Heather was probably the second best artist in the school. I started wondering what Sarah and the Leopards would hold up.

Everybody clapped. As Brian and Heather sat down Mr. McGregor welcomed the second pair.

"Go, Dragons!" somebody screamed from the crowd. A bunch of kids began to cheer.

I leaned in close to Tanner. "Will anybody be cheering for us?"

"I figure my brother will."

"I kind of like the Dragons," I said. "They would have got my vote."

They finished their presentation with a cheer, and the crowd started to clap. If the applause meant anything the Dragons had slain the Lynx.

That was two down, four more to go, and then us. I could hardly wait.

"And second to last, please welcome the Leopards," Mr. McGregor announced. As Sarah and Katie walked toward the microphone the lights dimmed. When the gym was completely dark, music started to play. From the back of the gym a beam of light shot out onto the screen beside the stage—a screen I hadn't even noticed.

On the screen a leopard, a big beautiful leopard, walked along and then leaped into a tree. The leopard photo faded and was replaced with a striking drawing of a leopard. I recognized the artwork—she *was* the best artist in the school. The scenes kept changing until the back of a school uniform appeared on the screen. It had the name Laggan on the top and a big number four—*my* uniform number. I knew that was a dig at me. Before our eyes the sweater turned around to reveal the front with a drawing of a leopard leaping across the jersey. Wow, it looked wonderful.

The projector light died, leaving us in complete darkness for a second before the gym lights came back on. Sarah and Katie were still standing at the podium.

"When you vote today, remember, think leopard, vote leopard," Sarah said.

"Go, Leopards!"

Everybody started to clap and cheer. I almost cheered. I could picture myself in that uniform. Who, other than Sarah, would have thought of doing a PowerPoint presentation?

"And now for our final presentation," Mr. McGregor said.

For a split second I'd forgotten we had to speak. How could we follow that?

"Please welcome Sam and Tanner."

chapter thirteen

I slowly got to my feet on unsteady shaking legs. My stomach was churning and for a split second I wondered if there was a garbage can in the corner where I could throw up.

I was pleased and surprised by the cheering. It sounded like a whole lot of people were on our side—not as many as had cheered for the Leopards but more than any of the other names.

"Come on," Tanner hissed, poking me in the ribs to get me to move.

We wobbled over to the podium, and Tanner stood in front of the microphone and started to talk. As he talked I looked out at the audience and then beyond them to the empty court and the basketball nets. I looked beyond the nets to the empty white walls. Most schools had banners hanging on their walls, banners celebrating team wins. Our walls were almost empty.

I felt a rapid rush of anger, then disappointment, then, strangest of all, satisfaction. We'd never won anything, but some of the happiest times I'd ever had were in this gym. It was one of my favorite places in the whole world. The more I thought that the better my stomach felt. I was going to miss being here. I was going to miss the people. I was even going to miss Mr. McGregor.

"And to conclude our presentation the captain of our basketball team, and co-chair of the Lard Butt campaign, would like to say a few words," Tanner said, and people started clapping again.

I knew what I was supposed to say. I had practiced it until late the night before. I also knew I wasn't going to say any of it.

"A few minutes ago I looked at that screen and thought about how good it would have been to wear that uniform, that Leopards uniform. Wasn't it beautiful?" I asked. I started clapping and the audience joined in.

I looked over at Sarah. She looked pleased but confused.

"And then I looked up at the walls. Looked around the gym." I paused. I knew people had no idea what I was talking about.

"Beautiful, clean, white walls. Most gyms have banner after banner hanging down from the ceiling, lining every wall. Banners for their championship teams, bragging about what they've done. Not our walls.

"We have a few banners. Mostly they're for participation in a tournament. No championships. No tournament wins. None. Not just for this year's teams but ever. The tradition of this school is not winning. But still, year after year, we put together teams and we go out there and try.

"What was that saying on the PA the other morning? A winner never quits and a quitter never wins. We never win, but we also never quit.

"We could wear those Leopards uniforms. We'd look pretty sharp. We'd have a cool name. But in the end, let's be honest: I'm not a leopard. I'm a Lard Butt." I paused. "And so are the rest of you. And I'm proud to be a Lard Butt. Go, Lard Butts. Thank you."

Tanner and I sat down to a round of applause. A bunch of kids—most of the basketball team and others—jumped to their feet. They were cheering almost as loud as they'd cheered for the Leopards.

chapter fourteen

The game was starting in less than twenty minutes. The Maple Ridge Mustangs were in the other dressing room. They'd breezed through their two play-off games. They must have been pleasantly surprised—make that completely shocked—when they heard we'd won against the only team that they couldn't beat. Because of us they were probably going to win the championship. I hated them.

"There's quite the crowd out there," Cody said as he came into the dressing room.

"I saw," Tanner said. "I guess I get my wish for a big crowd."

"I bet you'd like to take that one back, right?" I asked.

"Oh, yeah, in a second."

"Lots of parents out there," Cody continued. "I saw your mother," he said to Tanner and Taylor. "And your father," he said, pointing at me. I was happy my father was there, sort of.

Mr. Davidson and Mr. McGregor walked into the change room.

"Hello, boys," Mr. McGregor said. "I want a few words with you before the game."

We all sat up in our seats. This was the first time he'd talked to us before a game. I wasn't sure if he'd actually watched us play before.

"This is the first Laggan team to reach the finals in the six years I've been the principal here. Win or lose, this is the farthest any of our teams has ever gone." He paused. "Even the losing team receives a banner to hang on their wall."

Tanner and Taylor started clapping and

everybody joined in. Everybody except me. Was he writing us off as well?

"As you know we held the election for the new name yesterday. And, since the whole idea started with you boys, I want you to be the first to know the results."

Now he had my attention—all of it.

"It was a very close vote," he began. "In the end it came down to two names."

"Which two?" Tanner asked.

"Leopards and Lard Butts."

"Wow," I said under my breath.

"Wow, indeed, Sam. That speech of yours was very powerful. I noticed you weren't using any notes. Did you have it memorized?"

"It just came out of my head."

"And your heart, I would say," Mr. McGregor added.

"So who won?" Taylor asked.

Mr. McGregor smiled. He was enjoying this.

"One hundred and sixty-five votes were cast. That's every student and every teacher. Ninety-nine votes were split between the top two choices."

"How did Lairds do?" Taylor asked.

"Seventh place."

"Forget who finished seventh. Who won?" I asked.

"By a margin of fifty-one to forty-eight, the new name of the Laggan school teams is...the Leopards."

People groaned in disappointment. I didn't think any of the fifty-one votes came from this locker room.

"It was a close vote, and I know what name would have won if it was only the ten of you voting."

"We gave it a good shot," Tanner said.

"We just needed a few more votes. " Taylor said. "So close."

"Starting next year the school will be replacing its uniforms. You boys won't have a chance to be Leopards."

"I guess we're the last Lairds," Tanner said.

"You will be that, but you'll also be something else." Mr. McGregor opened a green plastic bag he'd carried in with him.

"They're not fancy, but I think you'll like

them." He opened up the bag and pulled out a white T-shirt. On the back was a large black number. He spun it around. On the front, in big letters, it read, *LAGGAN LARD BUTTS*. My mouth dropped open. I was stunned.

"I had them printed up just for this game, just for you boys. They're yours to keep after the game. A thank-you for a good season."

"I can't believe you did this," I said.

"Why not? Aren't you proud to be a Lard Butt?"

"That wasn't just a speech," I said. "I am a Lard Butt."

"It was a very good speech. And you know what, I'm a Lard Butt too."

He pulled out another shirt and held it up. It was identical to the others but in smaller letters in the corner was the word principal. He took off his glasses and pulled the T-shirt on over top of his dress shirt and tie.

"How does it look?" he asked.

"You look like a real Lard Butt," I said.

"And so do you, even without the T-shirt. Let me hand them out."

He pulled them out, one by one, reading

off the number and handing it to the player who wore that number. Player by player we pulled on our T-shirts.

"I think it's time we go out for our warm-up," Mr. Davidson said. He had on a Lard Butt T-shirt with *coach* written in the corner.

One by one the kids filed out of the change room until only Mr. McGregor and me were left.

"Thanks," I said.

"No, thank you," he said. "Things are going to be pretty boring around here next year."

"I could visit."

"That would be nice."

"Could I ask you a question?" I asked.

"Certainly."

"Who did you vote for?"

"Secret ballot," he answered.

"I know. I'm just curious. It wasn't Lard Butt, was it?"

He shook his head. "And it wasn't Leopard."

"Well, at least Sarah is going to be happy that her name won," I said.

"I'm sure she will. She put on a very good campaign. That girl will go far."

"Hopefully in a different direction then I'm going," I said.

"Maybe, maybe not. She's not the only one with potential."

"Me?" I asked.

"Don't look so surprised."

"It's just that Sarah is, you know, a cut above everybody else in the school," I said.

"She does have many talents. Shame she's such a suck-up."

My eyes opened in shock.

"Isn't that the word you kids are using these days to describe somebody who tries to get on the teacher's good side?"

"That's the word. I just didn't expect to hear it from you."

"And you didn't. I didn't say a word. Now, just go out there and be a Lard Butt."

"No problem. I'm a Lard Butt at heart and always will be."